A NOTE TO PARENTS

When your children are ready to "step into reading," giving them the right books—and lots of them—is as crucial as giving them the right food to eat. **Step into Reading Books** present exciting stories and information reinforced with lively, colorful illustrations that make learning to read fun, satisfying, and worthwhile. They are priced so that acquiring an entire library of them is affordable. And they are beginning readers with an important difference—they're written on four levels.

Step 1 Books, with their very large type and extremely simple vocabulary, have been created for the very youngest readers. **Step 2 Books** are both longer and slightly more difficult. **Step 3 Books,** written to mid-second-grade reading levels, are for the child who has acquired even greater reading skills. **Step 4 Books** offer exciting nonfiction for the increasingly proficient reader.

Children develop at different ages. **Step into Reading Books,** with their four levels of reading, are designed to help children become good—and interested—readers *faster.* The grade levels assigned to the four steps—preschool through grade 1 for Step 1, grades 1 through 3 for Step 2, grades 2 and 3 for Step 3, and grades 2 through 4 for Step 4—are intended only as guides. Some children move through all four steps very rapidly; others climb the steps over a period of several years. These books will help your child "step into reading" in style!

Library of Congress Cataloging-in-Publication Data
Hayes, Geoffrey. The treasure of the lost lagoon / by Geoffrey Hayes.   p.   cm.–(Step into reading. A Step 3 book)   Summary: Ducky Doodle realizes the true value of his friends Otto and Uncle Tooth when Sid Rat tries to cheat him. ISBN 0-679-81484-1 (pbk.)–ISBN 0-679-91484-6 (lib. bdg.) [1. Animals–Fiction.   2. Friendship–Fiction.]   I. Title.   II. Series: Step into reading. Step 3 book. PZ7.H31455Tr   1991 [E]–dc20 90-40118

Manufactured in the United States of America   10 9 8 7 6 5 4 3 2 1

STEP INTO READING is a trademark of Random House, Inc.

Step into Reading

THE TREASURE OF THE LOST LAGOON

by Geoffrey Hayes

A Step 3 Book

Random House 🏠 New York

Otto and his Uncle Tooth were on their way to see Uncle Tooth's sister. Her name was Auntie Hick, and they were going to paint her shop for her.

They saw Ducky Doodle outside the shop. Ducky Doodle worked for Auntie Hick. But right now he wasn't working.

He was sleeping!

Auntie Hick stuck her head out the door. "Doodle!" she cried. "Wake up!"

Ducky Doodle jumped to his feet. He quickly began sweeping.

"Hello, Doodle. Hello, Auntie Hick," called Otto and Uncle Tooth.

Just then Jiminy and Biminy
Weasel passed by. They laughed and
pointed at Ducky Doodle.

"His Pa was a famous pirate, but
he is just Auntie Hick's servant!" they
snickered.

"I'm nobody's servant!" yelled Ducky Doodle, and he stomped off.

Auntie Hick shooed Jiminy and Biminy away.

"I am worried about Doodle," she told Otto and Uncle Tooth. "I am trying to teach him to be good, but he thinks he should be tough. After work, he likes to go to Widow Mole's Pool Hall. I have warned Doodle about that place. It is full of thieves and troublemakers. I am afraid he will get into trouble too."

Otto thought for a minute.

"Maybe he needs someone his own age to do things with."

"I think you are right, Otto," said Auntie Hick.

Uncle Tooth said, "I will help Auntie Hick paint her shop. Otto, you can spend the day with Ducky Doodle."

"Oh boy!" said Otto.

He went around to the back of the shop. He saw Ducky Doodle sitting on a garbage can.

"Say, Doodle," he asked. "Do you want to go exploring with me?"

"No!" said Ducky Doodle.

"But we might find something wonderful," said Otto.

"I don't care!" said Ducky Doodle.

Otto sat down next to him.

"Doodle, if you don't come with me, we will *both* have to help Auntie Hick paint her shop."

Ducky Doodle frowned.

"All right," he said. "I'll go."

Auntie Hick fixed them a picnic basket. They took Otto's rowboat down the coast.

Soon they came to an old windmill.

"This would make a neat hide-out," said Ducky Doodle.

They went exploring in the windmill.

Otto found an old map of Boogle Bay. "This may be important," he said.

Ducky Doodle didn't find anything.

They went on. They passed under a bridge. Otto saw something stuck in the bank. He dug it out.

"A compass!" cried Otto. "I've been wanting one of these!"

Ducky Doodle looked, but he couldn't find anything.

They stopped at a little beach to eat their lunch. Otto found a pretty shell.

"I can give this to Auntie Hick," he said.

"It's not fair!" Ducky Doodle said. "How come *you* always find stuff?"

"Don't be a spoilsport," said Otto. "You just aren't looking hard enough."

"I am too!" cried Ducky Doodle.

The surf rolled out. Ducky Doodle saw something shiny in the wet sand.

Otto saw it too.

They both ran for it.

"It's mine! I found it first!" Ducky
Doodle said.

He dashed ahead of Otto and
grabbed it. It was only a bottle cap.

"I can't find anything good!" said
Ducky Doodle. He tossed the bottle cap
back into the water.

Suddenly, Otto stood still.

"What's that?" he asked. "It sounds like someone singing."

He climbed onto a tall rock and peered through his spyglass. "Maybe it's a mermaid."

When Otto turned around, he saw Ducky Doodle taking off in the rowboat.

"Hey! Come back here!" he called.

"I'll show you," answered Ducky Doodle. "I'll find something *really* good."

He steered the rowboat through a cave in the rocks.

Otto swam after him. It was dark and creepy in the cave, but Otto saw light up ahead.

He came out into a little lagoon.

"Wow!" said Otto. "A lost lagoon!"

"I found it first," said Ducky
Doodle.

"Maybe you did," said Otto.
"But you can't take a lagoon home to
Boogle Bay."

"I mean *this*," said Ducky Doodle.
He pointed to the water.

When Otto looked, he could see a sunken ship on the floor of the lagoon.

"Neat!" he said. "Let's go down and explore it."

"Not me," replied Ducky Doodle. "There might be swordfish down there...or the Creep from the Deep."

"I'm not worried," said Otto.

In a flash, he dove into the water and swam to the ship.

The ship had a big hole in its side.

Otto swam over the deck to the cabin.

Inside the cabin, he found an iron chest. On the chest was a brass sign that said *The Queen of the Sea.*

He tried to pry the lid open, but it was stuck tight.

Otto swam to the surface.

"This is a real discovery," he told Ducky Doodle. "Let's go home and get Uncle Tooth. We'll need a salvage boat. Good work, Doodle!"

Ducky Doodle grinned from ear to ear.

He helped Otto into the rowboat. They paddled toward the cave.

Then Otto heard the strange singing again.

"Listen...can't you hear it?" he said.

"Who cares?" said Ducky Doodle. "Let's go home and tell everyone about my discovery."

When they got back to Boogle Bay, they found Uncle Tooth painting the door of Auntie Hick's shop. Auntie Hick and Joe Puffin were watching.

"I wanted the color to be sea green," said Auntie Hick. "This is pea green."

"Green is green," said Uncle Tooth.

"Not to me it isn't," said Auntie Hick.

"Guess what?" Otto cried. "We found a lost lagoon!"

"*I* found it!" yelled Ducky Doodle.

"But I found the chest!" cried Otto.

"Tell us about it," said Uncle Tooth.

So they did.

"*The Queen of the Sea* was a famous trading vessel," said Joe Puffin. "She was lost in a storm way back when I was a lad."

"Do you think there's a treasure in that chest?" asked Otto.

Uncle Tooth lit his pipe and gave it a few hard puffs. "I wouldn't be surprised. Tomorrow morning let's all go and find out."

Ducky Doodle jumped for joy. "We're rich!" he said.

"Now, Doodle, don't get carried away," said Auntie Hick. She handed him a paintbrush. "There is still more painting to be done."

Ducky Doodle was too excited to paint.

When no one was looking, he slipped away down the street.

He went straight to Widow Mole's Pool Hall and ordered a soda pop.

Then he remembered he didn't have any money.

"I'll pay you tomorrow," he told Widow Mole.

Widow Mole frowned at him. "No pay—no pop!" she said.

"But I'll be rich tomorrow," Ducky Doodle said. "I just discovered a treasure."

"Fine. I'll sell you a soda tomorrow," said Widow Mole.

Sid Rat and Jiminy and Biminy Weasel were sitting at the next table. Sid Rat heard what Ducky Doodle said, and he smiled a wicked smile.

He walked over to Ducky Doodle's table. "If you found a treasure, you deserve a reward. Sid Rat is the name. Treating is my game!"

Sid Rat gave Widow Mole money for some sodas. He sat down beside Ducky Doodle.

Ducky Doodle was so flattered, he told Sid Rat all about the lagoon and *The Queen of the Sea.*

"So *you* found the lagoon and *you* found the ship," said Sid Rat. "But Otto and Tooth want all the credit. That's not right."

"No," said Ducky Doodle. "That's not right at all."

"Well, I'll tell you what I'll do," said Sid Rat. "I happen to have a salvage boat. If we take it to the lagoon early tomorrow, we can get the treasure first. And *you* will be the hero—not them!"

"Now, that's more like it!" said Ducky Doodle.

He did not see Jiminy and Biminy winking at Sid Rat.

The next morning, when Otto and Uncle Tooth were ready to leave, they couldn't find Ducky Doodle.

"Where could he be?" wondered Otto.

They waited a little longer and then headed for the lagoon. It was a perfect day for treasure hunting.

They had not gone far when they came to a sign that said DETOUR.

"I don't remember that from yesterday," said Otto.

"Are you sure we are going the right way?" asked Uncle Tooth.

They followed the sign. It led to a dead end.

"This is strange," said Uncle Tooth.

They had to turn their boat around and go back. Pretty soon they passed another sign: LAGOON THIS WAY.

"I thought you said it was a *lost* lagoon," said Uncle Tooth.

"Hmmm," said Otto. "I'm sure that sign wasn't there yesterday."

"Let's ignore it and see what happens," suggested Uncle Tooth.

They went on. Soon they passed the old windmill and the bridge. "We're getting warmer," said Otto.

Then he heard the strange singing again.

"What's that?" asked Uncle Tooth.

"I don't know, but it means we are near the lagoon," Otto said.

They came to the beach where Otto and Ducky Doodle had stopped for lunch. It was littered with empty soda pop bottles.

"I *know* these weren't here
yesterday," said Otto.

"I smell a rat," said Uncle Tooth.

They moored their boat and went
down the beach to the cave.

"Let's not go through it," Uncle Tooth whispered. "We can climb up these rocks and look over."

They climbed the rocks. When they got to the top, they could see the lagoon.

Sid Rat and Ducky Doodle were on a boat in the middle of the water. But where were Jiminy and Biminy?

"Surprise!" called Jiminy and
Biminy from behind them.

They flung a rope around Otto and
Uncle Tooth and pulled it tight.

"We've been expecting you," they
sneered.

They led Otto and Uncle Tooth
down a path to the water's edge.

"Howdy, boys," said Sid Rat. "First come, first served, I always say. We wanted to be here sooner, but Doodle kept getting lost."

"I did not!" cried Ducky Doodle.

"Doodle, you traitor!" said Otto.

"Now, boys, no fighting," said Sid Rat.

He turned to Ducky Doodle with a smile. "Since you discovered the treasure, I'm going to let you go down and fetch it. No sense in all of us getting wet."

Ducky Doodle shivered. "But it's dark down there. Maybe the Creep from the Deep lives in the lagoon."

Jiminy and Biminy broke into fits of laughter. "Oh, he's so tough!" they squeaked.

All at once, the strange singing echoed through the lagoon.

"See? I was right!" cried Ducky Doodle.

"You chicken liver!" said Sid Rat. "Go down before I push you down!"

"Leave him alone," said Otto. "I'll go. I know where the treasure chest is."

"All right," agreed Sid Rat. "But no funny stuff."

They untied Otto, and he dove into the water.

Sid Rat lowered a big hook from the side of the boat.

"Hook the chest on to this," he told Otto.

Otto swam down and slipped the hook under the handle of the treasure chest. Then he gave the chain a tug.

Sid Rat and the weasels cranked the chain. The chest rose to the surface.

But Otto did not follow. He swam toward the edge of the lagoon. Some light was coming from behind two rocks.

He headed toward the light and popped to the surface. He was in a grotto.

Parts of the ship were scattered all around. Otto saw the steering wheel, some plates and mugs…and best of all …a wooden figurehead.

"Why, she's beautiful!" gasped Otto.

Meanwhile, the weasels and Sid Rat were hauling the chest onto their boat.

"We're rich, boys!" said Sid Rat.

"Hey!" cried Ducky Doodle. "That's my treasure!"

"Not anymore, it isn't!" snarled Sid Rat. He pried the lid open.

The chest was empty.

"You lied to me!" said Sid Rat.

"And you lied to *me*," said Ducky Doodle. He ran forward and crashed into Sid Rat. Then he jumped overboard and swam to shore.

"Get the little squirt!" Sid Rat ordered Jiminy and Biminy.

Ducky Doodle ran along the shore of the lagoon. He came to a stone archway and hurried inside.

He found Otto in the grotto.

"Hide me," he cried. "The weasels are going to beat me up!"

Sure enough, Sid Rat and the weasels were right behind him.

Sid Rat stopped when he saw the wooden figurehead.

"The Queen of the Sea!" he said. "And look, boys, her eyes are made of jade!"

He pulled out a knife. "I'll just pop them out," he said.

"No!" cried Otto. "You can't hurt her!"

"Watch me," said Sid Rat. He started to climb onto the figurehead.

Just then she began to sing.

Sid Rat was so startled that he dropped to the ground with a thud.

"Ghosts!" screeched Jiminy and Biminy. They turned tail and ran.

Sid Rat ran after them.

All three ran right into Uncle
Tooth. He tossed a rope around them
and pulled it tight.

"No knot can hold Uncle Tooth,"
he said. "Sid, you and the boys are
headed for jail. I happen to know that
salvage boat of yours is stolen."

"Good work," said Otto.

Ducky Doodle was shaking with fright.

"Don't be afraid," said Uncle Tooth. "The wooden maiden isn't haunted. The wind blows through that hole in her mouth, and she sounds like she's singing."

They carried the wooden maiden out of the grotto.

Soon they were all on Uncle Tooth's boat, heading home to Boogle Bay.

The breezes sang through the wooden maiden's mouth as they went.

"Some adventure," said Ducky Doodle. "There wasn't even any treasure."

"What do you think the wooden maiden is?" asked Otto.

"But *you* found her. All I'm good at finding is trouble," said Ducky Doodle. He sighed. "I thought Sid Rat was my friend."

"You can't trust thieves," said Uncle Tooth. "If you spend your time with people like that, you will come to a bad end."

Ducky Doodle hung his head. "How do I come to a good end?"

"You can start by helping Auntie Hick more," said Uncle Tooth. "Do not be ashamed of an honest day's work."

Sid Rat and Jiminy and Biminy were put in jail for a week.

The wooden maiden was placed above the door of the Boogle Bay Museum. Uncle Tooth invited Ducky Doodle and Auntie Hick to come and see her.

"Isn't she cute!" said Auntie Hick.

"She's okay," said Ducky Doodle.

Otto was polishing a brass sign beneath the wooden maiden.

"What's that?" asked Ducky.

"Read it," said Uncle Tooth.

WOODEN FIGUREHEAD
FOUND BY OTTO AND DUCKY DOODLE
IN THE LOST LAGOON

"Wow! That's me!" cried Ducky Doodle. "I'm famous!"

The wind blew through the hole in the wooden maiden's mouth, and she sang a lovely song. The townspeople came over to listen.

"Otto and I found her," Ducky told everyone. "Isn't she beautiful?"

"Let's go exploring again tomorrow," said Otto.

"Sure thing," said Ducky Doodle. "After I finish my chores for Auntie Hick."

"My! My!" Auntie Hick whispered to Uncle Tooth. "He certainly is a different Doodle now."

Uncle Tooth puffed on his pipe and smiled. "A little adventure never hurt anyone," he said.